Five Spooky Ghosts Playing Tricks at School

SCHOOL

To Lois, the best sister *ever*!
–S.M.

For Laura and Matthew
–M.H-P.

ISBN 0-439-80381-0
Text copyright © 2005 by Steve Metzger
Illustrations copyright © 2005 by Marilee Harrald-Pilz
All rights reserved. Published by Scholastic Inc.
SCHOLASTIC and associated logos are trademarks and/or registered trademarks of Scholastic Inc.
12 11 10 9 8 7 6 5 4 3   7 8 9 10/0

Printed in the U.S.A.
First printing, October 2005

Five Spooky Ghosts Playing Tricks at School

by Steve Metzger
Illustrated by
Marilee Harrald-Pilz

SCHOLASTIC INC.
New York   Toronto   London   Auckland   Sydney
Mexico City   New Dehli   Hong Kong   Buenos Aires

Five spooky ghosts playing tricks at school.

One got wild and broke a stool.

The teacher called the mommy
and the mommy said,

"No more ghosts playing tricks at school!"

Four spooky ghosts drawing on the wall.

One stretched up, now he's too tall.

The teacher called the daddy and the daddy said,

"No more ghosts drawing on the wall!"

Three spooky ghosts
flying in the gym.

One tried to dunk and hit the rim.

The teacher called the grandma and the grandma said,

"No more ghosts flying in the gym!"

Two spooky ghosts using too much glue.

One got stuck and said, "Boo-hoo!"

The teacher called the grandpa and the grandpa said,

"No more ghosts using too much glue!"

One spooky ghost
bouncing in the yard.

Jumped up high and fell down hard.

The teacher called the doctor and the doctor said,

"No more ghosts bouncing in the yard!"

Now there are . . .
No little ghosts having fun at school.
No little ghosts breaking all the rules.

The teacher called the parents
and the parents said,

"Let those ghosts go back to school!"